To: . . . .

A magical story
for a magical you

From:

One sunny summer's morning . . . . was playing in her garden.

Suddenly she heard sniffling and crying coming from behind a leafy tree.

4

. . . .
tiptoed closer and closer
to the whimpering.

When she peeked around the tree
. . . . was shocked to see a
little white and purple, sad-looking...

5

UNICORN!

6

"Hello, my name is . . . ., what's your name and why are you **crying?**" she asked the unicorn.

7

"I'm Sparkle, and I've lost all the magic colors on my rainbow horn from giving out **too many wishes**," said the unicorn.

"That's terrrrrible!" exclaimed . . . . "HOW can I help you get your magic back?"

8

"Well," said Sparkle, "as I become happier color returns to my horn and when I have all seven COLORS my magic powers are restored and I can give out wishes again."

9

. . . . had a think, and a wonder and a ponder...

...what could she do?

"I've got it!" shrieked . . . .

"We need to do things that will bring back Sparkle's sparkle!"

#1

SO, they tried playing a game of hide-and-seek.

Sparkle wasn't very good at it but because she enjoyed the game so much the first rainbow color returned to her horn - ruby RED!

ching!

11

Then they sat on squishy
bean bags drinking hot chocolate
and eating rainbow-colored marshmallows.
This made Sparkle very happy!

slurrrp

With a slurrrp of her hot chocolate,
brilliant ORANGE flashed up on her horn.

"I know what you need
now," said . . . .

"...a PAMPER day!"

So they wrapped up in **fluffy robes**, had their **nails painted**, and were so thoroughly **pampered** that sunny

#3

YELLOW

pinged back on to Sparkle's horn.

13

#4 Next up on their fun-filled mission was bouncing UP and DOWN doing somersaults on . . . .'s trampoline.

They were having so much fun that Sparkle's emerald GREEN band reappeared on her horn.

#5 Hungry from so much bouncing, the two friends went inside to make unicorn shaped cupcakes.

14

There was flour and eggs everywhere when the color sky BLUE appeared on Sparkle's horn.

There were only two more colors to go and Sparkle was feeling SO much happier, but what could they do to get the last two?

"AHA!" exclaimed . . . ., as she remembered the **fun fair** had just come to town!

whizzed round and round and round on the last loop-the-loop Sparkle squeaked with suc

They zipped up and down,

16

...a bright INDIGO band appeared!

There was just one more color to go.

17

Exhausted from all the fun
the two friends settled down to a
magical film and some popcorn.
Sparkle was so happy that
bold VIOLET, the very last
rainbow color, popped
back on to her horn.

"That's it!
Thank you
. . . . !"
laughed Sparkle.
"You have made me
so happy that **all**
of my magical rainbow
COLORS have
reappeared and I can
grant wishes again."

"Now, what wish
would YOU like?"
asked Sparkle.
"I wish, wish, wish
I could see the
Unicorn Kingdom,"
. . . . said hopefully.

19

With a
ZING and a ZAP,
a WHIZZ and a WHIRL,
.... and Sparkle soared up,
up, up through the
wondrous rainbow.
Then in a flash
of twinkling pink light...

. . . . couldn't **believe** her eyes,
she was **really** there and all because she
had helped a **unicorn** have **oodles** of **fun!**

The End

COLOR ME IN →